Sally Loves . . .

TO SWIM!

Written and Illustrated by

Jody Mackey

Text and Illustrations Copyright © 2013 by Jody Mackey. 138712-MACK
Library of Congress Control Number: 2013912569
ISBN: Softcover   978-1-4836-6758-4
Hardcover   978-1-4836-6759-1
Ebook   978-1-4836-6757-7

Sally Loves...TO SWIM!: The compilation and subject, the format,
design, layout, and coloring used in this book are trademarks and/
or trade dress of Jody L. Mackey and ChampYouth, Inc.

This book may be ordered directly from the publisher, however, please try
your local bookstore first. Call us at 1(855) 529-2403 or see our full line of
products promoting active lifestyles and building confidence, for children at:

Website www.ChampYouth.com

Published by Jody L. Mackey

Rev. date: 08/26/2013

To order additional copies of this book, contact:
Xlibris Corporation
1-888-795-4274
www.Xlibris.com
Orders@Xlibris.com

May your dreams come true.....

To my Husband Don, whom I love endlessly. His seemingly, unlimited amount of encouragement in the pursuit of my dreams is extraordinary.
Thank you……..♥

Sally loves to swim.

Sally swims freestyle. Sally swims lap after lap in the big pool.

Sometimes Sally kicks with a kick board.

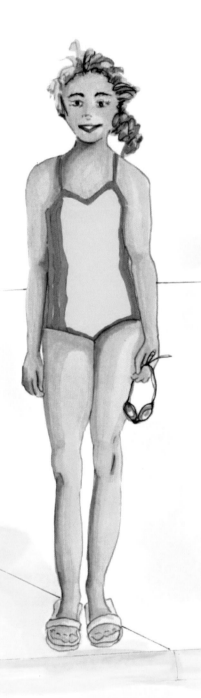

Sally wants to swim on the swim team with her brother Ryan. "The Swim team is fun, and you can do races with your friends!" says Sally.

Sally rides her bike to the pool every day
with her mom, and her brother Ryan.
Ryan has a red bike. Sally has a white bike.

"I wear my bike helmet every
time I ride my bike," says Sally.

Sally's brother Ryan loves to run.

Ryan runs really fast. Sally likes to
run with Ryan. Sometimes, Sally races Ryan on
the soccer field by the pool.

Sally's mom swims. Sally's mom rides her bike. Sally's mom runs in races. Sally's mom is a Triathlete!

Sally's mom races in triathlons and has lots of race medals.

"I swim, I can ride a bike, I can run fast,"
says Sally.

"Mom, I wish I could do a triathlon," says Sally.

"If you can dream it.... and if you work hard at it.... you can do whatever you set your mind to do," says Sally's mom.

All summer long, Sally swam with the swim team and Sally rode her bike extra hard to the pool. Sally ran with her brother Ryan, sometimes she even ran with her dog, Little Mack.

And then, Sally's mom signs her up
for a triathlon. Sally's best friend Cindy
is going to do the triathlon, too!

Cindy and Sally get race numbers.
They are so excited! Tomorrow is race day
and Sally can hardly sleep.

Sally's whole family gets up early to go to the triathlon. Sally's mom and Sally's dad, her brother Ryan and even, Little Mack gets to go watch Sally race.

Sally neatly organizes all her gear in the
transition area. She puts her bike right
next to Cindy's bike.

Cindy and Sally have their race numbers
marked on their arms and legs.

"Are you ready?" Cindy asks Sally. "I am
so nervous," says Sally. "You are a great swimmer!"
Sally says to Cindy. "You are so fast on your
bike!" Cindy says to Sally. "Good Luck!"
the best friends say to each other.

"Good luck!" shouts Sally's mom. "Have fun!" shouts Sally's Dad. "Go fast!" shouts Ryan. "Bark, bark.....bark!" says Little Mack.

Then, the buzzer goes off.... And the race starts!

Sally swims, Sally bikes, Sally runs and when she finishes, Sally gets a medal and a big hug from her mom and dad!

Even Little Mack is at the finish, with
licks and hugs!

Cindy finishes. Cindy gets a medal too! Sally and Cindy hug and say to each other, "I had so much fun. There is no one I would rather race with than you!"

'Sally Loves... you!'

Edwards Brothers Malloy
Oxnard, CA USA
October 24, 2013